THE MYSTERY AT Hilton Head Island

First Edition ©2017 Carole Marsh/Gallopade International/Peachtree City, GA
Current Edition ©October 2017
Ebook edition ©2017
All rights reserved.
Manufactured in Peachtree City, GA

Carole Marsh Mysteries™ and its skull colophon are the property of Carole Marsh and Gallopade International.

Published by Gallopade International/Carole Marsh Books. Printed in the United States of America.

Managing Editor: Janice Baker
Cover Design: Susan Van Denhende
Content Design: Susan Van Denhende

Gallopade International is introducing SAT words that kids need to know in each new book that we publish. The SAT words are bold in the story. Look for this special logo beside each word in the glossary. Happy Learning!

Gallopade is proud to be a member and supporter of these educational organizations and associations:

American Booksellers Association
American Library Association
International Reading Association
National Association for Gifted Children
The National School Supply and Equipment Association
The National Council for the Social Studies
Museum Store Association
Association of Partners for Public Lands
Association of Booksellers for Children
Association for the Study of African American Life and History
National Alliance of Black School Educators

Once upon a time ...

Hmm, kids keep asking me to write a mystery book. What shall I do?

Mimi

Papa said ...

Why don't you set the stories in real locations?

You sure are characters, that's all I've got to say!

Yes, you are! And, of course, I choose you! But what should I write about?

National Parks!

Scary Places!

Famous Places!

FUN PLACES!

Disney World!

New York City!

Dracula's Castle

GRAND CANYON

Write one about spiders!

We can go on the *Mystery Girl* airplane ...

I CAN FLY US ANYWHERE!

Mystery Girl

Or aboard
the *Mimi!*

Mimi

Take me to the
Forbidden City!

Or by surfboard,
rickshaw,
motorbike,
camel ...!

I can put
a lot of **history,**
MYSTERY, SCIENCE,
legend, lore, and **laughs** in
the books! It will be educational and fun!

Good
stuff!

LET'S GO!

And so, join Mimi, Papa, Avery, Ella, Evan, and Sadie aboard the *Mystery Girl*—where the adventure is real and so are the characters!

START YOUR ADVENTURE TODAY!
www.carolemarshmysteries.com

READ THE BOOK!

JOIN THE BOOK CLUB!

MEET THE CHARACTERS!

TRACK YOUR ADVENTURES!

1

THE HINKY DINKY

"There it is! There it is!" Avery, Ella, Evan, and Sadie shouted. They stood on the deck of the *Hinky Dinky*, a boat that ferried passengers from Palmetto Bluff across the May River and into the Calibogue Sound each day. What they had spotted on the shore was the famous red-and-white-striped Harbour Town Lighthouse.

"Is there anything prettier than a lighthouse?" Ella asked, her hair whipping in the breeze. Her grandmother Mimi nodded.

"Or more romantic?" swooned Avery, her eyes wistful. Mimi nodded again.

"Or *spooooooookier?*" suggested Evan, with a grin.

Everyone stared at the boy, who clasped the bobbing deck railing with white knuckles.

"Why spooky?" asked Ella in aggravation. "It's bright daylight and as far as I have ever heard, this lighthouse is not haunted." This time, Mimi smiled.

Avery looked startled. "Is it, Mimi? Is the lighthouse haunted?" She sounded hopeful.

"No!" Ella insisted. "Mimi brought us over to Hilton Head Island to have fun for a change—NOT to chase some ghost or mystery—right, Mimi? If you wanted to do that, you would have brought Grant and Christina." But Grant and Christina were getting older and had more important things to do this summer than solve mysteries (or so they said).

"Miiiiiiimiiiii?" Evan said in a teasing voice. "Tell us now. Tell us the truth."

Mimi stood on the bow of the boat, waiting for it to dock at the marina. She did not smile. She did not frown. She did not purse her lips the way she often did when she hesitated to tell her grandchildren something. Instead... she screamed!

2

PORPOISE SISSIES

"Where's Sadie?" cried Mimi. Her red sundress flared as she twisted left and right to look for her youngest granddaughter. "She was right here! She was walking Coconut." Coconut was Mimi's little white rescue puppy that she took everywhere, even on airplanes.

The children scattered to search for their five-year-old sister. Surely she had not fallen overboard? All the kids were good swimmers. Sadie could swim the length of their pool at home without taking a single breath.

Avery soon spied a glint of strawberry-blond hair bouncing in the breeze. Sadie stood with Captain Young at the stern of the boat. She squealed as dolphins jumped over the bow wake like wet, gray **parentheses**.

"Look! Look!" Sadie cried when she spotted her family heading toward her. "Porpoise sissies!"

"That's *porpoises*, Sadie," Ella corrected.

"They're manimals," Evan added.

"That's *mammals*," Ella corrected again. Evan stuck out his tongue.

"Besides," said Avery, "they are actually dolphins." Captain Young nodded in agreement.

"That's enough!" said Mimi, racing up to her granddaughter. "Thank you, Captain, but I'll take her from here." Mimi adored her four youngest grandchildren, but she found keeping up with them a handful. They never seemed to stay together in one place for long.

Sadie was so excited about the "porpoise sissies" that she let go of Coconut. The dog tore around the deck, dragging her red leash behind her.

Avery just stood there, **stoic**, ignoring the usual **ruckus**, and took in the scene before her. They were coming into port at the famous Sea

Pines, home of the also-famous Heritage Golf Tournament and the beautiful Harbour Town Lighthouse. As the noonday sun glinted off the waves, the green grass, the blue sky, and the storybook white puffy clouds, she sighed.

"Mimi," Avery said, tugging at her grandmother's arm. "This looks like a book cover to me. You did come here to write a mystery, didn't you?"

Now that everyone was accounted for, Mimi looked at her beautiful granddaughter and winked. "You don't think I came all the way over here on this lumpy-bumpy water just to eat lunch and shop, do you?"

Avery laughed. "No! But, uh, I sure hope we *are* going to eat lunch and shop."

"And climb the steps to the top of the lighthouse?" Evan butted in.

Mimi groaned. The one thing she could be sure of was that each of her grandchildren would want to do something different while they were at Hilton Head—and all of them would exhaust her!

With a jolt, the *Hinky Dinky* bumped into the wharf. Helpful deckhands tied the lines up to cleats. In a moment, the gangplank was lowered and they all walked, scampered, hopped, or skipped off the boat.

"That felt just like being a pirate!" Evan said, with that one-eyed squint he always had in the bright sun. "Made me feel just like Jack Wheelbarrow."

"Jack Sparrow," corrected Avery.

"No, Jack Bonemarrow," teased Ella.

"Where did the porpoise sissies go?" lamented Sadie, looking back at the water.

"DOLPHIN!" her brother and sisters yelled together.

Sadie folded her arms, stomped her foot, and ran to find Mimi, who was talking to Captain Young.

"Hey, you guys," Avery whispered. "Mimi said she IS going to write a mystery!"

Ella groaned. "And we are surprised?" She swiped her sweating forehead with the back of her hand.

"Then we'd better help her," said Evan. "You know she counts on us to..."

"To what?" asked Mimi, coming up behind them, hand in hand with Sadie and cradling Coconut in her other arm.

"Uh, to, uh...be good while we're here?" said Evan. His sisters giggled.

"Well, I could try to count on that," said Mimi with a sigh, "but I know better!"

Suddenly, Avery turned toward the town. "Do I smell hushpuppies?!"

Mimi laughed. "Was that sound I heard the sound of growling tummies?"

All four kids rubbed their stomachs and nodded.

"Then we'd better head to the Salty Dog right away!" Mimi said and herded the gang of kids forward off the dock and into the quaint village.

As the girls ran ahead, Evan lagged behind, muttering, "I don't want to eat a salty hot dog. I want shrimp and hushpuppies."

As usual, no one paid Evan any mind... except for the last passenger off the boat, who seemed determined to keep an eye on the young boy and his family.

3

THE SALTY DOG

The Salty Dog Café was just the kind of place the kids loved Mimi to take them to for lunch.

"Ah, outside tables with umbrellas," said Ella, as she plopped onto a deck chair.

"Aha!" said Evan. "I see fried shrimp and hushpuppies, and boy, am I hungry!"

The waiter took their order and the kids settled back; they knew what came next. Never, ever, had they gone anywhere with Mimi that she did not give them a mini-history lesson. It was never boring and often helped them solve the mystery that always seemed to be afoot.

Avery pulled out a map she had picked up at the front counter and unfurled it. She laughed. "Hilton Head looks like a foot!"

The other kids peered over her shoulder. The island was indeed shaped like a foot, with a heel, a sole, and a toe.

"And we are right here on the toe," said Ella.

"Can we go to Skull Creek?" begged Evan, pointing to another spot on the map.

"Where's the salty doggie?" asked Sadie.

"And why do they call it Hilton HEAD, when it looks like a FOOT?" Evan wondered aloud.

"Can I get one of those Salty Dog tees, Mimi?" pleaded Avery.

"Can I get my fingernails painted in red-and-white stripes like the lighthouse?" Ella asked.

Mimi ignored her grandchildren. She sat quietly, sipping her iced tea with lime and mint. When the kids grew quiet, she began.

"A *head* also means a point where land meets sea, especially where you can have a good lookout, say, for invaders. We're having *dinner* at Skull Creek. We *will* get tee shirts in the gift shop before we leave. And I *love* the idea of red-and-white-striped fingernails and toenails!"

As she spoke, the waiter brought their food, and ketchup was squirted all around. Sadie munched on her "salty dog" hot dog. While everyone ate, Mimi gave them some background.

"Hilton Head got its name from an English explorer—Captain William Hilton—who came here to map the coastline," Mimi explained. "His ship was called the *Adventure*. He spotted this point of land, which was named Hilton's Head, after him."

"And later, Hilton Head Island?" guessed Avery.

Her grandmother nodded and continued. "You've studied the 13 original colonies in school. Well, the colonists had to find ways to make a living. They built ships here, and later they established many plantations, where rice, cotton, indigo, and other crops were grown—with the help of slaves."

"Slaves?!" said Evan.

"I'm afraid so," said Mimi. "But after the Civil War, the slaves were freed. Hilton Head became a quiet island. People hunted, fished, and harvested trees for lumber. After a bridge was built to connect the island to the mainland, tourists began to come over to enjoy the wide, sandy beaches."

"Just like we do every summer!" said Ella.

"And they built the lighthouse so ships wouldn't run aground?" asked Avery.

Mimi laughed and nodded. "You can see its light 15 miles out to sea. But mostly I think it's famous because everyone loves it, and a famous golf tournament is played here each year—the Heritage. As a matter of fact, it starts soon."

"Can we go up in the candy cane after lunch?" asked Sadie, a ring of ketchup around her mouth.

"Yes, we can!" said Mimi, wiping Sadie's face. "And our history lesson will continue there."

The kids groaned.

With so many people in the café and tee shirt shop, it was not surprising that the kids did not spot the man from the boat still trailing them. While everyone else wore shorts and tee shirts and flip flops, the man looked out of place in his trench coat and slouch hat. In fact, he could not have looked more suspicious if he tried. And that made him *very* suspicious!

4

UP IN THE CANDY CANE

The kids thought they looked pretty cool in their new Salty Dog tee shirts—red for Evan, blue for Avery, purple for Ella, and pink for Sadie. Of course, Mimi had to snap a selfie of them all in front of the lighthouse. Then the kids raced toward the lighthouse.

Mimi decided to stay behind with Coconut. When she finally met up with the kids at the foot of the lighthouse, Mimi explained, "I don't think her little short legs can climb all those steps."

"Right, Mimi," teased Evan. "Blame Coco; it's OK."

Before his grandmother could argue back, the kids had turned and scampered up the steps as fast as they could. They only stopped for Sadie when she stomped her foot and squealed, "SLOW DOWN, you guys!"

To keep Coconut from charging after the kids, Mimi walked the little white dog around the base of the lighthouse. She never saw the shabbily dressed man follow her grandchildren up the steps. He didn't rush. He knew he had time. After all, once you got to the top, there was no place to go but down.

5

WHAT'S IN A NAME?

Mimi sat on a bench and looked at her map of Hilton Head. She loved the names she saw on the map—Windmill Harbor, Shipyard, Spanish Wells, Indigo Run, Palmetto Bay, Shelter Cove, Port Royal, Skull Creek, Honey Horn. She thought she loved the ocean, beach, and pirates as much as her grandchildren did. The kids thought she was writing a new Carole Marsh mystery book. They had no idea she was looking for a beach house to move to. And she could not tell them because they would NEVER stop screaming with glee.

When she heard someone call her name, Mimi got up and walked out away from the lighthouse. Shielding her eyes from the sun, she looked up to see the kids smiling and waving down at her. She was glad she'd bought them the brightly colored Salty Dog tee shirts so she could easily spot them in a crowd.

"How is it up there?" she cried.

"HIGH!" the kids screamed back.

"Help Sadie get back down safely," Mimi reminded them.

She returned to her bench and poured panting Coconut a bit of water into a paper cup. She went back to reading the map to plan out what they'd do the next few days. *Hmm*, she thought. *Would they like to visit some of the famous graveyards and cemeteries here? Or old plantation houses? Or Civil War ruins?* She laughed to herself, realizing those are the things that SHE would like to do!

Coconut gave a **WOOf**, and Mimi realized that the kids were taking an awfully long time to come back down from the top of the lighthouse. She stood and looked up the staircase but did not see them. Then she stepped back out onto the grassy lawn and looked up. Nothing.

"I sure don't want to march up all those steps, Coconut!" Mimi said. Coconut gave a bunch of **woof, woof, woofs** as the kids suddenly burst out of the lighthouse, breathless.

"What took you so long?" asked Mimi, relieved to see them.

"Oh, a man was asking us some questions. That's all," Avery explained.

"A man!" said Mimi. "What man? What did he want? Why did you talk to him? Wasn't he a stranger? Do you talk to strangers? You know you don't! You..."

"Calm down, Mimi, please," begged Avery. "It's all right. The man said he knew you. He just wanted to know what new book you were working on."

Mimi looked all around. "Do you see this man now? Has he left?"

Avery looked too. "No," she admitted. "But I'd sure recognize him if I saw him."

"Why is that?" asked Mimi, red-faced and trying not to show how upset she was. No one should be asking her grandchildren questions. And she doubted this man even knew her, or he would have asked the children where she was and come over to talk to her in person.

"Because even though it's so hot," Avery said, "he was wearing a trench coat and a hat." Her shoulders slumped. "I'm sorry, Mimi. You're right. We should not talk to strangers or believe everything anyone says, right?"

"Right, Avery!" said her grandmother, giving her a reassuring hug. "I am sure it was innocent, but I just worry about being responsible for you four rambunctious kids. Let's stick together and NOT talk to anymore strangers, OK?"

Avery smiled and nodded her head. The other kids stood up from petting Coconut and asked, "Now what?"

"I know we just got off a boat," Mimi said, "but it's such a beautiful afternoon. Let's go take a ride with Captain Amber so you can see those dolphins up close. Maybe you can even pet them!"

The kids squealed in delight. They loved the water and boats and dolphins. They had no idea that Mimi just wanted to get away from the area. She hoped to get the kids someplace where she could keep a better eye on them.

As they headed to catch the trolley, they never spotted the man who had stalked off across the golf course, a pen and notepad in his hand. He was so focused on what he was writing that he did not even notice a golf ball bouncing onto the green and into the hole beside his dusty shoe.

6

HEEL, TOE, HEEL, TOE

Mimi's friend "Car Wash Mark" had dropped her little red convertible off at Coligny Square, so they headed there to pick it up and drive to the dock where they could meet up with Captain Amber.

"Gee, the kids who live right here at the beach are really lucky," commented Evan.

"But they still have to go to school!" Avery reminded him.

Ella pointed at a yellow school bus and a crosswalk sign. "But after school and on weekends, we could swim, surf, walk on the beach, and do a lot of other cool stuff."

"I'd just like to live at the beach for the summer," said Avery.

"I'd love to go to school on an island," said Ella. "Even if I had to take the school bus over bridges over water."

"You got awful quiet," Mimi said to Evan.

For a moment, Evan didn't say anything. "Heel, toe, heel, toe, heel, toe," he began to chant.

"What does that even mean?" asked Ella.

Evan sighed. "I'm just trying to figure out how far it would be to walk around this entire island."

"We'll ask Captain Amber," Mimi suggested, as she pulled into a parking spot by the dock. "She knows everything about the Lowcountry."

"This is the LOW country?" asked Sadie. "Lower than me?" Everyone always teased her because she was the shortest in the family.

"I thought Hilton Head was still in America," said Evan.

"It is!" Mimi laughed and explained, "They call the coast from Savannah, Georgia, all up South Carolina and into North Carolina the Lowcountry because so much of it is at sea level."

"That's pretty low," Evan agreed.

"Especially in the storm surge from a hurricane!" said Avery. Hilton Head and the surrounding area had been hit by Hurricane Matthew recently, and the kids remembered the photographs of the devastating damage Mimi had shown them.

"That's true," said Mimi, herding the kids toward the dock. "But at least you have a warning that a hurricane is headed your way, and, if you are smart, you evacuate!"

"Like you and Papa did when you came to Aunt Michele's house?" asked Ella.

"Coconut, too!" reminded Sadie.

"Yes," said Mimi. "It was the safe thing to do. Plus, we had a lot of fun. It was like a mini-vacation since we were high and dry."

Evan rubbed the back of his hand across his brow, which slung a little sweat Avery's way. "Oooh, Evan!" she complained.

"It's getting hot. I'm thirsty," he said.

Mimi shook the small ice cooler she carried. "Lemonade! Now get on board and don't embarrass me by acting like a bunch of hooligans!"

The kids giggled. "But I thought that was our job!" Avery teased. Mimi just shook her head.

Onboard, they all settled into their places. Every place was filled but one. Captain Amber said hello and gave a brief safety talk and helped the kids get into their orange PFDs.

"PFD?" said Evan, pointing to the block letters printed on his life jacket.

"Personal Flotation Device," explained Captain Amber, reaching for a small one for Sadie. Coconut cowered in Mimi's lap, and Mimi tightened her hold on the red leash.

"Don't worry, Coco," said Ella. "No MOB on this trip."

"MOB?" asked Evan, wondering what language they spoke on Hilton Head.

"Man Over Board," said Ella.

"That's right!" said Mimi. "NO one overboard; got that, Evan?"

Evan made a face. "Why are you guys picking on me? I can swim, you know. Besides..."

Suddenly, Evan's face grew pale as a ghost crab. They all turned to look behind them. Running down the dock was The Man in the trench coat. He had his hat pulled down close over his face. He hopped in the boat and took the last seat. The kids gasped.

Captain Amber looked up and said, "John, you almost missed the tour. Put this on." She handed him a life jacket, released the lines from their cleats, and pushed the boat out into the water for their tour.

7

THE MAN EXPLAINED

As soon as they were underway, Mimi scooted close to Captain Amber and whispered, "You know him?"

Captain Amber kept her eye on the water as they eased out into the channel. "Sure," she said. "He's a reporter for *The Sandpaper News*, the local newspaper. He often comes aboard when there's an extra seat to see what's up on the water or look for a good story."

"Well, I think the story he is looking for is me," Mimi grumbled and frowned. Her grandchildren looked worried, and leaned forward in their seats to put distance between themselves and the strange man.

Suddenly, the man stood up and walked toward Mimi. This caused the boat to rock a bit, and the kids squealed. He stuck out his hand. "Caught in the act!" he said, shaking Mimi's hand when she finally offered it.

"Sit down, John; you know the rules!" ordered Captain Amber.

"Sorry," the man said and quickly returned to his seat. "I didn't mean to seem to stalk you," he apologized. "I just wanted to be the first to get a story about your new mystery book set at Hilton Head."

Mimi gasped. "But I haven't even written it yet! Besides, why didn't you just call me and set up an interview?"

The kids followed the conversation like it was a tennis match. Their heads flew back and forth from the reporter to their grandmother.

"I tried!" the man admitted

"You did not; I never got a call," Mimi returned

"Maybe your cell phone service is iffy? Mine always is."

"You could have emailed!"

"I didn't know your email address."

"So you just followed me—us—even up into the lighthouse?"

The kids had never seen Mimi quite so aggravated.

"Well, I wanted to surprise you."

Suddenly, the man removed his hat and to the kids' surprise, Mimi looked shocked. "I know you!" she said.

The man was much younger than they had thought. He gave a boyish grin. "Yeah, I'm..."

"I know who you are!" Mimi repeated, shaking her head as if she still couldn't believe how he had tricked her.

"WHO IS HE?!" the kids begged.

Mimi laughed. "He's John! He was a character in my first mystery book."

"*The Mystery of Blackbeard the Pirate*?" guessed Evan.

"Yes," said John. "I was just about your age. I met your mom and dad, who were the other characters. Of course, they were kids too, back then. We had a lot of fun. Your Mimi dragged us all over town doing research.

We mostly behaved, but every time we did something silly or sneaked off up into some attic, and even into a fireplace, she ended up putting that in the book."

"Did you meet Blackbeard?" asked Evan.

"Sure did!" said John. "But more importantly, I met a real-life author. And that made me want to grow up and become a writer, which I did—and am!"

Mimi shook her head again. "Well, I declare, I just don't know what to say. I'm glad to see you—I think!" She pointed to her grandchildren. "This is my current batch of real characters."

"Oh, I know," said John. "I've read all about them. I teach fourth grade here on the island when I'm not reporting. That's one reason I wanted to get an interview. I promised my students that I would meet Carole Marsh—or die trying."

"Uh," interrupted Avery. "Mimi does not like for us to use the *die* word. Not when she's working on a mystery."

"I'M NOT WORKING ON A MYSTERY!" Mimi blurted with a pout.

Everyone laughed. They all knew Mimi better than that!

John leaned in toward them and whispered, "Well, there *is* a real mystery on the island. Maybe you can help me solve it. It's actually pretty serious."

Mimi thought YOU meant her, but the kids felt sure John meant THEM. They sort of liked this John. Maybe he could help too, they thought.

But right now, Captain Amber reminded them all that they had come on her boat to see the marine and bird life. "So why aren't you looking at it?" she asked. "And by the way, Sadie, take those tasty fingers out of the water, sweetie, so the fish won't nibble on them!"

"Or gators or sharks!" Evan whispered to Avery and Ella.

The other kids glanced at each other in alarm. "Are there really sharks in these waters?" Ella asked.

"Of course," said Captain Amber, "and alligators."

"Wow," Avery whispered to Ella and Evan, "a stranger who turns out to be a book character, a real-life mystery, an island, sharks, and gators—this is gonna be a fun mystery!"

8

SHARKS AND GATORS

Before long, the kids had forgotten all about any mystery—fiction or real—as they became enchanted by all the wildlife on the water and the many things that Captain Amber told them. She pointed out a regal blue heron standing proudly on the shore and egrets white as snow on a sandbar. A beautiful green-and-yellow sea turtle surfaced near the boat and she told the kids they could reach down and touch its glistening shell. A pod of dolphins making *clicking* sounds jumped alongside them. White caps caused the boat to bob around a bit. On the mudflat edge of the marsh, a large alligator slid into the water with a plop. But they never did see a shark.

"But one *could* have seen us," Evan reminded them later.

Captain Amber told them about the giant megalodon teeth fossils that had been found in these waters. "That's a gigantic prehistoric shark!"

"I just want to see some fish jump," said Ella. No sooner were the words out of her mouth, than a large fish with glistening scales arced up ahead of them. They all laughed.

"This is such a magical place," Mimi said. Everyone grew quiet.

GRRRRROOOOOWWWWWLLLLLLL! Evan's stomach gurgled so loudly that everyone heard it and burst out laughing. "Well, I just want to EAT a fish," he said.

Captain Amber brought the boat about and they headed back to the dock. "Me, too, Evan," she agreed.

As she tied up the boat and put the PFDs away, the others climbed onto the dock and tossed their empty lemonade cans into a green recycling bin.

"We're going to dinner at Skull Creek," Mimi said to John. "Would you like to join us later?"

John grinned. "I hoped you'd ask me! That would be great." As he opened the car doors for them all, he whispered, "And I'll tell you about the real mystery then, OK?"

Mimi frowned, but the kids nodded.

They got in the car, buckled up and headed to their beach cottage. As soon as Mimi drove off, Sadie and Coconut fell asleep in the back seat. Quietly, the other kids conspired about how they could get away from Mimi and start solving a mystery!

9

REAL-LIFE MYSTERY

The kids' parents were staying at Mimi's house in Palmetto Bluff. But because Sadie and Coconut were so tired, Mimi asked them to pick up some dinner and bring it to the cottage and spend the night.

Later, they were surprised when Mimi said she felt bad—"Too much sun?"—and wanted to stay home, too.

Fortunately, John said he would take them to The Boathouse at Skull Creek for dinner and get them back safely. Since he was a teacher and a former book character, both Mimi and their parents agreed.

"That way we can go and hear about the mystery without any interference," whispered Avery to her brother and sister.

And so, the kids soon left Mimi napping, their mom and dad cutting pizza for Sadie, and Coconut curled up in her little pink bed in the corner.

"It's like we're the adults!" said Evan as they left the cottage and piled into John's big red Jeep.

"Not hardly!" he reminded them. "Buckle up and behave! I don't want to get in trouble with your Mimi or your parents. So a nice quiet dinner and an early evening, OK?"

Avery, Ella, and Evan nodded eagerly, but Evan whispered, "And MYSTERY for dessert!"

The Boathouse was one of their favorite places. They had eaten there often with Mimi and Papa. A beautiful sunset was sinking into Skull Creek. The last of the shrimp boats to come in were tying up at the docks. John got them a table by the water beneath a large outdoor fan and beside some flaming tiki torches.

"Boy, this is the life!" said Evan, sprawling back in his deck chair.

"Island life!" John said in agreement. "Hard to beat, even if I do have to work two jobs to make ends meet."

"Hey," said Ella, "that was sort of a poem."

"Well, tell us the mystery!" Evan insisted, cutting right to the chase.

"Can we order first?!" grumbled Avery.

They did. As soon as a large basket of hushpuppies was delivered to their table, Ella asked, "Why do they call them hushpuppies?"

John, now in jeans and a tee shirt that read WILL WORK FOR GOLF, answered in his teacher voice, "One theory is that during the Civil War, when soldiers would sit around the campfire, they'd cook a cornmeal kind of dumpling in the fire. To keep their starving, barking dogs quiet so they would not give away their location to the enemy, they'd toss these nuggets to them, saying, "Hush, puppy!"

The kids liked that answer. They quietly sat for a moment, thinking about the story and munching their own hushpuppies.

"See, it works," John said with a wink.

"Are there places on Hilton Head where we can learn about its history?" Avery asked. She was the history buff of the family.

"The Coastal Discovery Museum is a great place to visit," said John. "I take my students there on a field trip each year. They have regular exhibits and ones that change, so we never know what we might see and learn."

"Well, how about jumpy houses and putt-putt golf and ziplines?" asked Evan. "That's more my style."

"Plenty of that, too," John admitted.

"What about this mystery you promised us?" said Ella. She sounded irritated. "Or are you just making it up?"

John remained silent while the waiter put their food in front of them. It was as if what he had to say was for their ears only. And since the kids were hungry, he had their full attention as they ate fish and crab and shrimp, washed down with sweet iced tea.

At last, the teacher/reporter let out a big breath. "OK, here goes," he began. "You guys might think a beach town's just all about vacation and sun and fun. But, really, Hilton Head's just like any other place—good guys and bad, problems, police, politics, and all that kind of stuff.

"When I was doing a story recently on the upcoming Heritage Golf Tournament—which is a big deal here—I started getting some weird emails.

"I know to you kids, a golf tournament just sounds sort of boring, but this is part of Hilton Head's tradition. It brings a lot of money to the island. There are a lot of volunteers and some pretty famous golfers come to play."

"So?" interrupted Avery. "What's the problem?"

John hesitated. "I'm not sure. But the emails were a bit threatening. At first, I thought it was about me. I thought someone was jealous that I got to do the story. But since my wife is about to have a baby, I didn't want anyone coming around trying to pick some fight with me."

Ella frowned. "But now you don't think it's about you?"

John shook his head. "Not really. The more emails I got, the more it sounded like someone just wanted to mess up the golf tournament. I don't know how or why, exactly, but it scares me."

"You mean like cheat, or something?" asked Evan. Papa told him being honest in golf was important, just like being honest in life.

John shook his head again. He hesitated for a long time.

"What is it you don't want to tell us?" Avery asked. Her stomach sort of hurt as she sensed John's anxiety. *What could be so bad?*

"OM-GOSH!" shouted Ella. She hunched down and repeated in a much softer tone after everyone stared at her. "Oh my gosh...you don't mean the T-word, do you? Please say you don't!"

John sighed. "I shouldn't have even started telling you guys this. You're too young."

"What T word?" asked Evan. "Like T-Rex?"

Avery had caught on to John's fear. "No, Evan," she said softly. "Like *terrorism*."

"No way!" said Evan. "That's just on the news, not here in paradise, right?"

When no one answered him, Evan looked scared.

"No, no, Evan!" John said. "I really don't think that, but..."

"BUT???..." the three wide-eyed kids said at the same time.

"What I mean," John said, "is not guns and bombs, but maybe someone just up to no good, just to cause problems, just to mess up other folks' fun."

Avery snapped her fingers. "Or," she said, "as a cover-up to something else they want to do that's wrong!"

John stared at her like she was a genius. "That's brilliant!"

Avery shrugged her shoulders. "I've been around Mimi a long time," she said.

"Sooooo," said Ella, "some dude wants to cause trouble just for fun, or he is just pulling your leg, or..."

"Or dudette!" said Evan. "*Girls* can be bad too, you know."

John laughed. "You should know, Evan. You have a lot of sisters!"

Evan groaned. "Don't I know it, John, don't I know it. Hope your new baby is a boy."

"It is!" John said. "We just found out!"

The kids cheered and high-fived John. Then everyone grew quiet.

"John," Avery finally said, as the sun sank down below the purple horizon, "I don't think Mimi would want us involved in this kind of mystery. It could be dangerous."

"Yeah," agreed Ella. "Her kind of mysteries are more like, uh, made up, you know—fiction. Not the kind that ends up on the front page of your *Island Packet*."

John nodded. "I agree, Ella. It's just that..."

"Just what?" Ella asked.

John smiled. "It's just that the dude—or dudette—sent...*CLUES.*"

"CLUES? CLUES?!" squealed Evan. "Well, why didn't you say so? Clues are what we are good at!"

All the kids nodded, so John spread the emails out on the table.

10

CLUES GALORE

"Wow!" said Evan. "That's a lot of clues all at one time. Usually we struggle to solve clues one at a time."

Ella gazed at the mass of emails and sighed. "I don't think we're here long enough to figure out what all these clues mean," she admitted.

Avery was very quiet. She stared at the clues. "Maybe," she said, "this person is just trying to confuse you. Otherwise, why so many clues? After all, the tournament has already started."

"True," said John, paying the bill, "but it's not over until Friday."

"So we have some time!" Evan said.

"Yeah, but we'd have to get away from Mimi," warned Ella. "And that's never easy!"

"John," Avery said with an adult tone in her voice, "we'll help you as much as we can, but we can't get into any danger or anything like that. In our world, mysteries are supposed to be more like fun and figuring things out. We don't want to do anything that will get us hurt."

John threw up his hands. "I understand!" he said. "I don't either. I don't even want you to help. You're just kids. Your grandmother may be writing a mystery book, but it's not THIS mystery. I just thought you might have some ideas that I could pursue on my own."

Avery, Ella, and Evan looked at each other. Finally they smiled. "And leave us out of all the fun?" Avery said. "I DON'T THINK SO!"

And so, reluctantly, John gave the kids the file of emails for the night. He figured no harm would come to them if they took a look.

All the kids piled into John's Jeep and headed to the cottage. No one said a word all the way back. John figured the kids were just tired, or maybe worried, like he was. But when he turned around after he parked in the driveway, he saw the kids hunkered over the emails, already trying to solve the mystery!

Oh, dear, he thought. *What have I done?*

11

SLEEPY TIME DOWN SOUTH

By the time the kids got in, Sadie, Mimi, Mom, and even Coconut were all sound asleep.

"You guys sure are home late," Dad said. He did not look too happy.

"It's OK, Daddy," said Evan. "John fed us good and got us home safely."

"It's not even eight o'clock," Avery mumbled under her breath.

"But I think we really want to go to bed, too," said Ella with a big yawn.

The other kids looked at her like she was crazy, then quickly caught on.

"Oh, yeah!" Yawn.

"Me, too!" Yawn!

"What a day! Night, Dad. You look pretty tired, yourself."

Their father just shook his head. He knew something was up, but he had no idea what. But his kids going to bed early was all right with him. He could sneak into the Man Cave and watch an old *Star Trek* movie. So he hugged them all goodnight, and they ran to tuck themselves in. *Kids*, he thought. *Go figure!*

Sadie was sleeping with Mommy. Mimi's door was closed. Dad had vanished for at least two hours with the rest of the pizza into the Man Cave. *Dads, go figure*, the kids thought.

Avery, Ella, and Evan quickly put on their pajamas, brushed their teeth, and gathered in the bunk bed room. Once they were convinced that they would not be interrupted, they spread the emails on the floor and hovered over them with a flashlight.

"Weird!" said Ella, after they had read over the clues at least twice. "Read them out loud,

Avery, and let's see if they make any more sense to us."

Avery stacked up the emails/clues and read them aloud:

Cannon you find me?

It's just a blimp on the horizon.

See you later, alligators!

Man, a Tee!

Horseshoes are so crabby!

A Tacky Marsh, or a Marsh Tacky?

A Calibogue

Plaid Nation

A Crazy Crab

The Lady in Blue; now that's a *real* clue!

"OK, you guys, figure them out!" she challenged.

Exhausted, Ella and Evan looked at their sister like she was crazy.

"You gotta be kidding!" said Evan.

"There's no way we can figure these out," Ella agreed. "At least not anytime soon."

"We can do anything we set our minds to," Avery reminded them. "Mimi taught us that. So let's get started, but, maybe in the morning?"

The other kids nodded lazily at that idea, and then they all collapsed into a heap of troubled sleep.

12

BLUE GOOSEBUMPS

The next morning, their mom slept late; so did Sadie and Coconut. The other kids were up early, determined to solve the mystery so they could get to the beach. But it soon became clear that the clues were all too confusing to sort out into anything that meant something.

"I think if I had a peanut butter and jelly sandwich and a swim, I could figure out these clues a lot better," said Evan with a big yawn. The kids had gotten little sleep.

While they hoped John would show up to help them, he must have been in school, "or writing on a deadline for the newspaper?" Ella wondered.

"Don't say the D-word," Avery reminded her. "We don't need any jinxes."

"We don't need anything except..." Evan hated to admit, "Mimi to help us."

The kids thought about that a minute, but they knew that if they told Mimi anything about these clues, they'd be banned from doing any sleuthing. So instead, they made those sandwiches and headed for the beach.

Their dad was already standing knee-deep in the waves, so they knew it was OK for them to go ahead and swim. The water felt wonderful, cool enough to be refreshing, and warm enough not to give them goosebumps.

"Help you do what?" Mimi startled them by asking. She had come up behind them and they never heard her over the crashing waves.

With big eyes and his fingers crossed behind his back, Evan said, "SURF!"

Mimi laughed. "Well, a surfboard might help!"

"Uh, BODY SURF!" Ella said.

Now Mimi laughed hard. "That's a good one," she said. "When's the last time you saw me body surf?"

The kids looked surprised. "Uhh, last time we were at the beach!"

Mimi blushed. "Oh, yeah. I forgot about that. Well, swim for a minute, because John is coming to pick you up. I have some, uh, work to do, and your dad needs to run back to Palmetto Bluff. John called and said he had the day off and wanted to show you around—isn't that nice?"

"Nice?" screeched Evan. "It's a miracle!"

When Mimi looked puzzled and a bit suspicious, Ella pushed her brother into the waves. "Surf, Evan—now!"

Mimi shook her head. "No hurry, guys. Just come back up to the house after your swim and get dressed." She turned and walked down the beach, picking up seashells that had washed ashore with the last tide.

As soon as she was out of sight, the kids motioned to their dad that they were going in. They made a dash for the beach house.

When Avery stepped out of the warm water into the cool air, she shivered. She glanced at her arm and said, "Goosebumps!"

13

CANNON YOU FIND ME?

"I think these clues are like a scavenger hunt," John speculated. They sat in Skillets Café and Grill in Coligny Square. He had learned that if he fed these voracious kids they seemed to focus better on the task at hand—just like his students! He was always bringing cookies or cupcakes to class to tempt them into learning history with more enthusiasm.

Avery frowned, a skim of pancake syrup atop her upper lip. "Usually when we go on a scavenger hunt, it's because we have one clue...and then where it leads us is to another clue. We've never gotten all the clues at once."

"You'd think maybe they didn't want us to actually solve the mystery?" wondered Ella.

Her biscuits and gravy sat congealing on her plate like beached jellyfish.

"Then what would be the point?" asked John.

Evan waved a piece of toast in the air. "The point would be we need to get started scavenging!"

"True," said Avery. "It won't take long for Mimi, Mom, or Dad to track us down to do something, you know, *educational*."

John sat back in his chair, pretending to be offended. "Would that be so bad?"

The kids laughed. "On vacation, it would!" Avery said. "We just had all our tests, you know."

"Did you pass them?" John asked.

"Better than we are doing passing this test," Ella grumbled, poking at the clue list with her sticky fork.

"I don't intend to flunk Mystery!" Evan declared.

"Then let's get on the road—or off the road," said John. "I brought the Jeep today.

We can go by land, water, up the side of a lighthouse, or..."

This made the kids laugh. "Go big or go home!" Ella said.

Before long, the sleuths were zipping along the fairly empty early morning roads of Hilton Head Island. The girls loved the wind blowing their hair around. Evan put his arms up in the air like he was riding a roller coaster. Even John grinned like a big kid. He had his GPS set for a Civil War fort.

"Sounds too educational to me," Avery complained.

"Sounds like there might be CANNON!" Evan said.

"Drive faster, John!" urged Ella.

Instead, John started teaching. "Before Hilton Head was covered with vacation homes, it was speckled with forts," he explained. "Because the island is so large, and strategically situated, it was important to the defense of the South Carolina mainland."

John pulled into Fort Howell and parked the Jeep on an oyster shell path, which made a sound like crunchy breakfast cereal.

A sign read:

FORT HOWELL
built by
U.S. Troops- 1864

OPEN DAYLIGHT HOURS
Hilton Head Island Land Trust, Inc.

"Where's the fort?" asked Evan, looking around at the scraggly forest.

John sighed. "Gone with the wind! But when Union forces took Hilton Head in the Battle of Port Royal, more than 1,000 African Americans became some of the first freed slaves of the Civil War."

"Wow, that is historic!" said Ella.

"I don't see any cannon," Avery noted. "But you can still see the outlines of the earthworks."

John smiled. He stared at the historical site. "Close your eyes, kids," he said softly.

They did, and he let them listen to the wind in the pines and the live oaks and the Spanish moss for a few moments. "See the fort back in time in your imagination," John said. "The walls are up, the soldiers are bustling; you hear cannon fire in the distance. Sense their bravery and fear. They are trying hard to protect the islanders, willing to give their lives. Smell the smoke. Hear the urgent commands. A battle is about to ensue!"

Evan gasped. "Were you here?"

John laughed and the kids opened their eyes. "I'm not that old! But the way to enjoy history—and not just learn about it—is to imagine YOU WERE THERE. Think with your emotions; listen and touch and smell and feel with your senses."

"I think I just touched poison ivy," said Ella, scratching the back of her bare leg.

"What about the cannon clue?" asked Avery. She was hot and sweaty and ready to move on if there was nothing to see.

"There it is!" shouted Evan.

The others stared where he pointed but could not understand what he meant. Evan marched up to an informational sign and pointed to a black cannon drawn on it.

"I guess that'll have to do," John agreed. He took a picture of it with his cell phone. "It isn't much to go on, but time's a'wasting—let's move on."

CRACK! The snap of a twig caused them all to turn, startled at the sound. But it was just a young deer, apparently curious as to what the humans were up to this morning.

"Yeah, let's go," said Evan. He was beginning to feel the ghosts of times past, and that made him nervous. Evan quickly pulled the list of email clues from his pocket. Next to the word "Cannon," he wrote a big checkmark.

14

JUST A BLIMP ON THE HORIZON

When they got back onto the main road, the traffic had picked up.

"Where are all these people going?" asked Ella.

"Why aren't they at the beach like we would be if we didn't have to solve this mystery?" asked Avery.

John laughed. "People aren't just piling onto Hilton Head for vacation. They're coming in for the famous Heritage Golf Tournament," he explained. "There will be a lot of famous golfers here and a lot of events going on."

It sounded pretty boring to the kids, so they just nodded, until Evan suddenly shrieked, "LOOK! Overhead!"

While the others craned their necks to see what Evan was talking about, he went on and on. "It's gotta be the world's biggest drone! It's humongous! Big as a dinosaur! A whale!"

"Big as a BLIMP, Evan," Avery corrected her brother.

"A what?" asked Evan, excited.

"A dirigible," added John. He pointed straight up.

Ella looked up out of the top of the open Jeep. "It says MET LIFE."

"That's better than MET DEATH," joked Avery.

Evan crossed his arms and tucked his hands under his shoulders. He grimaced. "You guys are confusing me. I spot a giant drone, and all you can talk about are blimps and diri...diri..."

"Dirigibles," John finished. "An airship. Like the famous *Hindenburg* that hit a tower and crashed and burst into flames in 1937."

The kids stared at the enormous airship floating above them. "Are we in danger?" asked Avery, throwing her arm over her head.

"Oh, like your arm will protect you," said Ella, giggling.

"We're fine," John assured the kids. "The Met Life blimp is here to cover the golf tournament for television. See that small compartment beneath the blimp?"

The kids peered hard at the belly of the blimp beast.

"Yeah," said Evan. "Is that its..."

John chuckled. "It's where the drivers of the blimp sit to control it, to fly it."

"Well, I wish they'd fly it a little to the left of us," grumbled Ella.

"I wish the big drone would drop some pizza right here in my lap," said Evan, holding his hands high, palms up.

"It's not a drone," John said. "It's sort of like a big helium balloon. That's why they call it an airship. That compartment has cameras beneath it. When you watch the golf tournament on television and see overhead close-ups of the course and the players, that's where the pictures are coming from."

The kids thought about that for a moment as the airship floated away, dragging its whale-like shadow with it. Hot sunshine spewed back down onto their heads.

"So it's sort of a *spy* ship, right?" Evan asked. *And another clue to check off my list,* he thought.

"You could say that," John said, knowing that was the answer Evan wanted to hear.

The kids glanced around at each other. As they well knew, that was something to tuck away in their mystery-solving brains.

15

SEE YOU LATER, ALLIGATORS

John took a gravel back road to their next stop. As they bounced along in the Jeep, the kids admired the island landscape that they loved to visit.

They passed giant live oaks with what Mimi called "old man's beard"—Spanish moss—dangling from the low-hanging branches. The long limbs of the trees were festooned with Resurrection fern, so named because it seemed to be brown and dead until it rained, when it automatically turned bright green once again.

On each side of the road were long, narrow lagoons filled with water the color of coffee.

Avery asked if they could stop so she could take a picture. Slowly, John pulled over to the side of the road and parked the Jeep.

Quietly, the kids hopped out of the Jeep, taking care not to slam their doors.

"It's like being in church," Ella whispered.

"Sort of haunting," Avery agreed, walking ahead to look for a good shot.

"It looks like a good place for..." Evan began, then screamed: "ALLIGATORS!"

The girls scampered back to the car. John herded them close to him. "No crying wolf, Evan," he warned.

Evan pointed. "No wolf," he whispered. "Gator...big one...at twelve o'clock."

Sure enough, dead ahead in the dark shadows by the closest lagoon, an enormous alligator appeared to be sleeping. He lay half in and half out of the water. His head was as big as Evan's skateboard and his scutes were as large as shark teeth.

The kids huddled close to the car and each other. Bravely, Avery lifted her cell phone and took a picture. As soon as the phone made a clicking sound, the alligator responded by zipping out of the water. It sped toward them, standing tall on its bent elbow legs, eyes wide open, teeth glimmering in the sunlight.

The kids squealed loudly, but just as soon as the gator got out of the water, it suddenly settled back down on its belly and slowly closed its eyes.

"I guess it thought it was dreaming," John said. "I hope you guys learned a lesson."

"Like what?" asked Evan. "Who thought we'd see a real, live alligator?!"

"There are a lot of them around," John said. "This is their natural habitat, you know. They were here first. We are the visitors."

"I learned to watch better where I'm going!" said Avery, scrambling into the car.

"I learned it's good to go to the bathroom before you get to gator land," said Ella, and they all laughed.

As the kids settled down and their hearts quit racing, Avery asked, "How do people get along, living alongside gators? I've seen them on the golf courses, too."

"There are rules to living with wildlife," warned John as he pulled the Jeep onto the road. "Watch out for it, stay clear of it, and whatever you do—DON'T FEED IT!"

"Why not?" asked Evan, craning his neck to see if the gator was following them.

"It's not good for the alligators," explained John. "They don't want to mess with people, and they don't want people to mess with them. If you feed them, and they get too friendly, they might have to be relocated—or even killed."

"That's terrible!" said Ella.

John nodded in agreement. "It is. So respect the wildlife."

Evan tapped John on the shoulder. "But we might need to be friends with an alligator," he said softly.

"No way!" said Ella.

"Why?" asked Avery.

Evan looked out the back window once more. "Because. It's one of the clues!"

As John and the girls boisterously disagreed about needing to meet up with another alligator, Evan ignored them and whispered to the wind, "See you later, alligators..."

Evan reached for his list of clues. *Where could all these clues be leading us?*

16

MAN, A TEE

As they came out of the maritime woods and back onto a main road, the girls spotted a gift shop.

"Stop, John, stop!" they shouted, beating on his shoulder.

"What? What?" he said, not understanding. "Not another gator, I hope?"

"No," said Ella. "We want to go to that cute gift shop right there, the one with all the tee shirts hanging out front."

"Are those twenty-dollar bills Mimi gave each of you burning holes in your pockets?" John asked and laughed.

"Of course!" said Avery.

Evan poked his fingers down into the pockets of his cut-off jeans. "Not mine," he said, puzzled. "No holes here!"

John pulled off the road. "I'll get some water bottles. You kids shop, but I am not kicking in any extra, so stay in budget," he warned.

The kids hopped out, and before long each had made their purchase. Avery picked out a tee shirt with a pretty horse on the front. She loved horses. Ella chose a tee with pink and purple seahorses all over the front. That was the kind of "horses" she liked. And Evan bought his shirt at a different register and went into the dressing room to change. When he came out, he stalked across the shop, chest out, with a big grin on his face.

"Evan!" the girls squealed. "Yuck!"

"Man," said John, "a tee shirt only guys could love." He and Evan exchanged high-fives.

Evan's shirt caught everyone's eye. It had a great white shark on the front, or at least its big, gaping mouth and giant teeth dripping with blood. The bottom of the shirt was ripped into jagged edges, also blood-tinged. It was funny and scary, and a bit too realistic, all at the same time.

"Now that everyone looks so spiffy, let's run by the Boathouse again and get some lunch," John suggested. Everyone agreed and dashed to the Jeep.

At the Boathouse, the diners couldn't stop staring at Evan. He loved the attention. The girls loved the feel of fresh, new tee shirts. And they all loved the scent of frying fish wafting from the kitchen. John picked a table by the boathouse, where small boats arrived and fishermen cleaned their catch on the dockside table, tossing the guts into the waters of Skull Creek.

As soon as they ordered, the kids got down to business.

"This is a lot of fun, John, but I don't think we are making much progress on the mystery," Avery announced.

"That's because there IS NO MYSTERY!" said Ella. "There was sort of a mystery with a weird-looking guy following us—sorry, John!—but it turned out to be you, so mystery solved."

"I don't think so," said Evan. "What about all these clues?"

Avery slumped on the table. "What about them? They don't mean anything and they don't lead to anything."

"Yeah," said Ella, twirling her long hair around her fingers, the way she did when she was anxious. "What's a mystery without a mystery? We might as well go to the beach."

"Aw! No!" said Evan. "We always solve the mystery, when there is one, and if there's not one, well maybe we can make one up or..."

"EVAN!" the girls fumed. "We are going to the B E A C H!"

While they'd been arguing, John grabbed a newspaper off the next table and read the front page. He looked worried. "Maybe not," he said.

"Maybe not what?" asked Avery.

The waiter showed up with their food and the kids were quiet as he put down their shrimp baskets and lemonades. "Cool shirt, dude!" he said to Evan with a wink. Evan beamed. The girls groaned.

Before they could dig into their food, John turned *The Sandpaper News* around. "Maybe there IS a mystery," he said.

The kids gaped at the huge headline: HILTON HEAD LIGHTHOUSE THREATED WITH A BOMB?

"Whoa," said Evan. "That's serious."

"Tell me about it," said John. "The island is packed with tourists and golfers. This could be a catastrophe!"

"Well, we might as well go to the beach," said Avery, stuffing a shrimp into her mouth and crunching down. "Mimi will definitely not want us working on any mystery related to a BOMB!"

"But it just says MAYBE," said Ella, slurping her clam chowder. "John, read the article, please."

As the kids munched French fries, John read the article to himself, mumbling off and on, and then stopped to explain. "Well, it says there was some kind of threat, a note, about a bomb and a lighthouse...this weekend...so it could be a hoax...or..."

"Or a reason Mimi won't let us continue to work on the mystery we're working on," insisted Avery.

"What mystery is that?" asked Ella. "I don't see any mystery yet?"

"Oh, there's a mystery all right," said Evan. "We know we have a mystery because we have CLUES!"

Avery swiped her brow and sighed. "Oh, Evan, I think we are on a wild goose chase."

Evan was excited. "Then let's find the wild goose! We can't give up!"

John patted Evan on the arm. "I think the girls mean this is a ruse, Evan. The clues lead nowhere. Just like this bomb threat probably does too."

Evan folded his arms and frowned. "Well, I don't give up that easy! One mystery, two mysteries, bring 'em on! Mimi would be disappointed with us if we quit, wouldn't she?"

Avery and Ella nodded. "Yes, but she always wants us to be careful," said Avery.

"And she doesn't even know we're working on a mystery," Ella reminded him.

Evan waved his arms around in frustration. "Well, you all just go on to the beach and get sunburned. I'm going to keep chasing clues and geese and whatever there is to chase. Maybe the e-mail mystery and the lighthouse bomb threat mystery are related."

The others looked surprised. "It's possible," John admitted, "though remote, Evan, very remote."

Evan looked satisfied. "Well, hand me the remote and I'll change the channel to the Mystery Channel. Let's get back on the case, you guys!"

His enthusiasm was infectious. The girls, and even John, hopped up and raced to the

Jeep. Evan followed, but he was biting his lip. Why? Because he knew he had NO IDEA WHAT he was talking about. *Oops.*

17

HORSESHOES ARE SO CRABBY

They ran by the beach cottage to make sure neither Mimi nor their parents were looking for them. But no one was home. They weren't on the beach either.

"Maybe they went out to lunch," Ella guessed.

"Oh, well, let's go for a swim while we're here and cool off," Avery suggested.

"You guys do that. I need to run by the newspaper office," John said. He spun around and left before the kids could ask him any questions.

"I think he wants to go check on this bomb threat thing," Evan said.

"I hope he comes back to get us before Mimi or Mom and Dad show up and put us to work babysitting Sadie or something," Ella remarked.

At that thought, the kids quickly changed into their swimsuits, grabbed towels, and headed for the beach.

It was a beautiful sunny day with a light breeze. Storybook clouds paraded across the horizon. The Atlantic Ocean was calm with small whitecaps and nice riding waves. The kids grabbed their boogie boards and jumped on them, speeding along on the shallow surf. They knew their parents wouldn't want them to get out in the deeper water without an adult around.

But there were adults around, and a lifeguard on a tall white chair, and a lot of kids and babies and dogs...everyone enjoying vacation fun.

"How come we have worries?" Evan said. "We're just kids."

Ella splashed her brother. "Because," she said, "we grew up helping Mimi solve mysteries, and now we're hooked. We can't resist."

"And you think she depends on us?" asked Avery, slinging her long wet hair around.

"I certainly do!" said Evan. "She can't do it without us."

Ella smiled at her brother. "I sure hope NOOOOOOTTTTTTTTT!" Ella shocked them by screaming and hopping around on one foot, and then the other, struggling to get out of the surf and onto the beach.

"What's wrong, Ella?" pleaded Avery, looking all around.

"Sharks?" asked Evan hopefully.

"SOMETHING! I DON'T KNOW WHAT!" Ella squealed.

And then they spotted the horseshoe crab Ella had stepped on. It was brown and round with a bony shell and a long, skinny, pointed thing sticking out the front.

Evan laughed. "I think you scared it, Ella."

Ella sputtered salt water. "I scared it? It scared me!"

"It's just a horseshoe crab, "Avery told them. "It's beautiful, except that when you turn it over it looks like a giant spider."

Ella squealed. "Horseshoes are so crabby!" she insisted.

"At least it's not a jellyfish," Evan said, shuddering.

"Or a stingray!" added Avery.

They heard a SPLaSH and nervously turned just in time to see John splashing into the waves. "The ocean is a living thing," he reminded them with a laugh, having watched the event from shore. "Just like those gators, the fish and crabs, and even the sharks, were here first. We're playing in their sandbox."

Evan looked around. "You mean bathtub, don't you?"

John laughed. "Hey, you guys, go get cleaned up real quick. We're going to see something special. But we have to hurry."

As the kids ran to the house to change, Ella called back, "This special thing doesn't have legs, does it?"

John nodded and smiled. "Oh, yes, indeed. It sure does!"

And as Evan raced to keep up with the girls, he mumbled to himself, "Horseshoe crab—another checkmark on the list!"

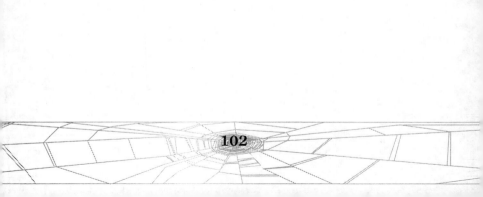

18

A TACKY MARSH, OR A MARSH TACKY?

John would not tell them where they were going, which drove the kids crazy and then him crazy with their endless questions. He refused to answer except to say, "Just wait and see!"

Soon he pulled the four-wheel-drive Jeep onto a sandy section of beach the kids had never seen. A long line of people stood at the edge of the dunes watching the water. At the far end of the beach, they could see a flurry of activity.

"Horses!" exclaimed Avery. "Look over there—on the beach!"

"Yes! They're Marsh Tackies," John explained. "Those small, sea island horses came here 400 years ago with Spanish explorers and traders. They adapted to their new environment and worked to plow the land, pull up stones, and even deliver mail."

"And..." Ella interrupted, "HERE THEY COME!"

The kids stood mesmerized as a string of beautiful brown ponies sped past them, kicking up sand, their riders holding tightly to the reins, until one crossed the finish line down the beach.

"That was exciting!" said Avery. "I wish I could ride a Tacky Marsh."

"A Marsh Tacky," John corrected.

"Yeah," said Evan, "a tacky marsh is one filled with litter." He cringed. Once, Mimi had taken them on a beach clean-up. It was awful to see how much trash had been dumped in the marshes and dunes.

John started back to the car. "Well, that was the final race. I thought you kids would really want to see it."

"Because we love horses?" Avery asked.

John grinned. "Nooooo. Because 'Marsh Tacky' is one of your clues! Who's solving this mystery anyway?"

The girls gasped. They realized that they'd gotten sidetracked from the mystery clues.

Evan pulled the clue list from his pocket. "Hey!" he exclaimed. "I've been keeping up with the clues! See?" Evan lifted the checked list high in the air.

Avery smiled at him. She was proud of her little brother. "Well, then, now we'd better figure out what a Calibogue is!" she said.

"Sounds like some kind of boogeyman to me," said Ella with a shiver.

"As in, 'the Calibogue is gonna get you!'?" teased Avery.

"Hush, Avery," Ella said. "You're kind of scaring me."

No one was really scared. The kids were only teasing each other like they always did. They just didn't know—yet—that there might indeed be something to be scared of!

"No one needs to be scared," John said, as he pulled into the parking lot at Sea Pines, right near the lighthouse.

"Well, here we are again," said Evan. "With no more mystery than we had before when that guy was following us."

"That guy was me, remember," said John. "But at least now you have a clue list, and I have an answer to clue number seven."

They hopped out of the Jeep, stood on the dock, and gazed at a glistening blue body of water.

Avery snapped her fingers, "The Calibogue Sound! Of course. We crossed it when we came over here on the boat, right?"

"Right!" said John, ordering them all iced tea and motioning for them to sit at one of the wooden picnic tables by the water.

"And now we're in for the lecture," Evan moaned. "You adults are all alike."

John ignored him. "The Calibogue Sound is a really cool waterway. It's 13 miles long, shaped sort of like a dolphin, and in some places is nearly 70 feet deep!"

"What does its name mean?" asked Ella.

"It's a Creek Indian word that means 'deep spring,'" said John. "It's filled with wildlife—bald eagles, wading birds, shorebirds, oysters, great blue heron, bottlenose dolphins, and loads of fish like red drum, Spanish mackerel, tarpon, whiting, and more."

"And people!" said Ella, waving her arm at the scene before them. The sound was filled with boats of all kinds going this way and that. A regatta of tiny sailboats with white sails looked like birds frolicking on the water. The ferry boat from Daufuskie sped by, leaving a rooster tail of water spewing behind it. The wind whipped up whitecaps on the sparkling blue water.

The kids spotted a pod of dolphins near the dock. They also spotted an adventurous young man with a pack on his back being pulled by a speedboat. When long tubes filled up with water from the sound, it shot up into the sky. "Look at him!" Evan exclaimed. "Where do I sign up for that?!"

Sea Pines was equally busy with golfers, photographers, tourists, reporters, security, and broadcasters. "Looks like they're keeping a good eye on the lighthouse," Ella noted.

"I don't think they're letting people inside the lighthouse right now," John said.

When the kids looked, they could see that he was right. There was an area **cordoned** off to keep visitors a certain distance from the lighthouse. People looked unhappy, but safe was better than sorry.

"Today's newspaper will say that article about a bomb scare was most likely a hoax," John said.

Avery gave him a funny look. "Who wrote that article, anyway?"

John blushed. "I did," he admitted. "I went in early and wrote it before I picked up you kids. It was not a big deal, at least not at six a.m. That's why I was so surprised to see the big headline over the story. I guess I needed to come see for myself that everything's going along more or less normally."

"AND IF IT HADN'T BEEN?" a voice behind them boomed suddenly.

They all gasped and whipped around. "Mimi!" screeched the kids. John looked like he might faint. Mimi glared at him.

"Hi," he said sheepishly. "I really did call ahead and hear it was all clear except for the lighthouse being off limits to climbers today," John promised. "I didn't want to upset you. The kids were just trying to figure out clues to the mystery."

Mimi's green eyes grew very wide. Her blond curls sticking out from beneath her straw fedora jiggled. *"Mystery?"* she said, glaring at John. "MYSTERY?!" she repeated, startling her grandchildren. "THERE IS NO MYSTERY! I HAVEN'T WRITTEN IT YET! THERE ARE NO CLUES!"

Mimi put her hands on her hips, and the kids couldn't figure out if their grandmother was going to yell some more or cry. Instead, she grabbed them all in a big hug. Holding the group tightly, she sort of dragged them along with her over to a café table and ordered, "Sit down!"

"Boy, are we in trouble now!" Evan whispered to his sisters. All the kids knew: YOU DON'T WANNA MESS WITH MIMI!

19

PLAID NATION

"We're sorry!" Avery and Ella said together. "We didn't mean to upset you, Mimi."

"Me, either!" insisted Evan, not wanting to get in trouble.

John wisely kept his mouth shut.

Mimi bowed her head and pulled them down close to her face. "Shhhhhhhh!" she warned. "Just listen!"

They all got quiet, even a little afraid. What was wrong?

"There IS a mystery," Mimi said. "Only not the one I'm writing. I've hardly had time to write at all. That's why I wasn't home when you came back to swim."

"Wait. How did you know we went back?" asked Evan. He believed that adults had eyes in the back of their heads and could see everything kids did.

"Evan!" said Mimi. "Uh, wet bathing suits on the kitchen counter...wet towels on the floor..."

"Oops!" said Ella. "Sorry, we were in a hurry."

Mimi shook her curls. "When are you kids not in a hurry?"

"Well, we're never in a hurry to do our homework," admitted Evan with a grin.

Mimi sighed. "Shhhhh. Listen. There *is* a mystery. There was a threat to bomb the lighthouse at Hilton Head—only not THIS lighthouse!"

"What?!" John said. He looked stunned.

Mimi explained. "After you wrote your article and left, more news came out, only the police insisted it not be shared. They don't want people panicking."

"It all looks pretty calm here," said Avery, glancing around.

"Yes," said Mimi. "And that's what we want. But the truth is..." She leaned in closer and so did the kids. But just as she spoke, a marching band of bagpipers rounded the corner and blasted their way past them.

"THIS MUST BE THE PLAID NATION?" Evan screamed, but no one heard him. Not only did the band wear red tartan plaid tams and kilts, but so did many of the tourists, golfers, and those running the tournament. It was indeed a "Plaid Nation." Even dogs had tam'o'shanters bobbing on their heads, and tiny kilts around their backsides.

The kids watched the parade until it passed. In the meantime, Mimi had told John what was going on. He looked like he'd seen a ghost.

By the time the kids turned back around, John was gone. Mimi herded the group to her shiny black SUV.

Her grandkids were not afraid of much, not ghosts, or mysteries, or dark nights, or—well, they were afraid of all that—but not nearly as much as they were afraid of...

MAD MIMI!

20

A CRAZY CRAB

Surprisingly, Mimi was not mad at all. She was hungry; so were the kids.

"We are going right to Crazy Crab for dinner before it gets so busy that we can't get a seat for sunset!" she said.

Sunset was a big deal on Hilton Head. The sun often turned the sky and water into brilliant ribbons of red and gold. But the kids were more interested in hushpuppies and John's whereabouts.

"Is John coming?" Avery asked, as soon as they were seated at a sunset table.

"No," said Mimi. "He had some work to do back at *The Sandpaper News*. Maybe you'll see him tomorrow."

"Where are Mom, Dad, and Sadie?" asked Evan. "Are they coming?"

Mimi shook her head. "No, Evan. They headed back to Bluffton."

"To get away from danger?" Ella wondered aloud.

"No!" Mimi insisted. "To...to..." Mimi seemed lost for an answer. Finally she said, "They had some paperwork to do."

The kids looked at each other doubtfully. Their parents never did "paperwork." All their work was computer work. Besides, this was vacation. Sadie did more paperwork than anyone, coloring on everything in sight any chance she got. But the kids knew better than to argue.

Instead, they enjoyed a lovely dinner of fresh-caught fish, salad with home-grown tomatoes, and hushpuppies. Then Mimi treated them to hot fudge sundaes.

"So," said Evan, his blue eyes twinkling, "what did the hot fudge say to the ice cream?"

"Tell us," replied Mimi. She loved to hear Evan's jokes.

"See you next Sunday!" Evan announced. His sisters giggled and Evan grinned from ear to ear.

After their dessert, Mimi let the kids play on the beach with the glow-in-the-dark bracelets and necklaces she had gotten them. It was so much fun to be invisible except for the neon colors flickering on your arms and neck! They couldn't even tell who was who since there were a lot of other kids out in the dark having the same kind of fun.

On the way back up the beach, someone bumped into Evan. Instead of apologizing, the mysterious person thrust a note into his hands and ran off. Evan stuffed the note into his pocket and ran as fast as he could to the cottage.

"Well, I'm surprised you kids are so eager to go to bed!" Mimi said. "I thought we might watch a movie."

But the kids all yawned and stretched and swore they were "just exhausted." It sounded curious to their grandmother, but she was tired herself, and so everyone headed to different rooms. Soon it was quiet and the lights were out...

...but not in the kids' bedroom. The kids huddled on Evan's top bunk with a blanket over their heads and a dim flashlight turned on. There they studied the message given to Evan on the beach.

21

A SHORE THING

The note said:

YOU KIDS AND YOUR
REPORTER FRIEND AND
YOUR GRANDMA BETTER
STAY OUT OF MY BUSINESS,
IF YOU KNOW WHAT'S GOOD
FOR YOU!

"Are you sure you didn't see this person's face?" asked Avery.

"How does he—or she—even know who we are? We are just here minding our own business on vacation," Ella said.

"No and no," answered Evan.

"No and no what?" Avery asked with a groan. "This is not the time to be silly."

Evan switched off the flashlight and shoved the blanket off of them. They sat in the dark with only the glow sticks visible around their necks and wrists. Anyone peeking in the window would just see disembodied lights.

"I'm serious," Evan said. "No, I did not see the person who handed me the clue. And no, we are not just here minding our own business. Everywhere we go we talk mystery and clues, and anyone could overhear us. Maybe this person heard us at the lighthouse earlier tonight."

"You have a point," said Avery, the light band around her neck bobbing. "Maybe we are closer than we think to solving the mystery. Maybe we are making them nervous."

"It's never good to make the bad guys nervous," said Ella, her voice quivering.

"We're just kids," Evan reminded them. "We're harmless."

Avery's headband bobbed again, spewing rainbow colors onto the dark walls. "But they don't know that. They know we know a reporter. They know our grandmother has a reputation for solving mysteries. I think they are just trying to scare us off."

"So and so," said Ella.

"So and so what?" asked Evan, exasperated.

"So," said Ella, "are we going to be scared off? And, if not, so what are we going to do next?"

The kids were quiet.

Finally, Avery snapped her fingers. "I have an idea," she said. "I'm going to turn on the lights." The bed bounced as she hopped up.

"NO!" squealed Ella and Evan. "Mimi will see that we're not asleep."

"Mimi won't care when I tell her what I'm doing," Avery assured them.

Suddenly there was another loud **SNAP**, but it wasn't Avery's fingers. It was their grandmother flicking the light switch.

"Just as I figured!" she said. "You kids are not in bed. Your feet are still sandy. And you're still wearing glow stuff, not pajamas!"

"It's OK, Mimi," Avery said calmly. "I was just about to get up. I have something important to do."

Mimi looked suspicious. "What?"

Avery couldn't help herself—she smiled a tiny smile. "Homework. I have homework, summer homework, and it needs research. I'm in the mood to do it now."

Mimi—as well as the other kids—looked surprised. But Mimi nodded. "I understand," she said. "Go on then. Are these characters helping you, or can they go back to bed?"

Now Avery gave a big smile. "They can go back to bed," she said, giving a dismissive wave of her hand. "I don't need them."

Before Ella and Evan could argue, Mimi rushed them off to the bathroom to clean their feet, change clothes, and get back to bed. She smiled fondly at Avery and said, "You can use my computer if you need to. It's downstairs. I'm going back to bed myself." With a big yawn, she left the room and padded across the hall.

Amidst the sound of splashes, giggles, and slapping towels, Avery slipped out of the room and went downstairs.

An hour later, Avery gasped when four hands clamped down on her shoulder. "What's going on?" she demanded. "You kids are supposed to be in bed."

"You really thought we'd stay upstairs?" Ella said. "That was a mean trick, sister."

"Yeah," said Evan. "You threw us under Mimi's bus; thanks a lot!"

Avery laughed. She tossed her long hair. "Sometimes a big sister just can't help herself, guys. Sorry!" She turned back to the computer. "Sit down. I really do have an idea and now I have some information and a supposition to share with you."

"What's a susso-pition?" asked Evan. "Is it anything like pizza, because that's what I'd like to share right about now."

"A supposition is a notion, an idea, a speculation—I have one about the lighthouse," said Avery. "Sit down and listen and then we'll make pizza—quietly."

"Don't worry," said Ella. "When Mimi smells the cheese bubbling, she'll be up to join us!"

"I can wait," Evan grumbled. "But not for long. Just look at this!" Like he always did when he was hungry, he lifted his pajama shirt and sucked his stomach in as hard as he could—so hard that his pants almost fell off. He had to grab them with one hand.

"Funny!" said Ella. "But you won't starve in the next five minutes. Sit."

They gathered around Avery's hunched shoulders and looked over at the computer monitor.

"There's more than one Hilton Head lighthouse," she explained. "I just couldn't figure out why someone would want to bomb the pretty—but not real—red-and-white lighthouse down at Harbour Town. Also, I couldn't figure out why the police presence was so light down there after the threat. Just a little yellow crime scene tape around the base, and people all around. It didn't make sense."

"What other lighthouse?" asked Ella. "I haven't seen another one around."

Avery pulled up an image. A strange-looking tall tube surrounded by a long skirt of criss-crossed poles appeared on the monitor.

"It looks like a tall skeleton," said Ella.

"Or an alien spacecraft," added Evan.

"It's a lighthouse," Avery promised. "The tower is 90 feet tall. That thing on top is the lantern room; it's made of cypress and has a reflector light. It has 112 steps in that six-legged skeleton!"

"So this is the *real* Hilton Head Light?" Ella asked.

"Yes," said Avery. "It's the real thing that kept ships from crashing on shore. It even survived an earthquake in 1886 and lots of hurricanes too. And..." Avery pursed her lips. She seemed unable to finish her comment.

"And what?" asked Ella, nervous and suspicious.

"It's said to be haunted! To have a ghost. The Lady in Blue!" Avery finally shared.

"Cool!" Evan said. "It's about time we came up with a mystery and a ghost and an alien skeleton lighthouse!"

Avery punched her brother in the arm. "It's not funny, Evan. This is probably the lighthouse the bomb threat is about. If it got demolished, that would be the end of some pretty important local history."

"It looks really old," Ella said, "like it could fall down all by itself?"

"Where is the ghost?" asked Evan. "Way up at the top?"

Avery sighed in exasperation. "I don't know the answer to any of these questions! I just know that we—and maybe everyone else— is looking at the WRONG lighthouse!"

"And the clock is TICKING," Evan intoned dramatically.

Ella shook her head. "Isn't it always?!"

"And," Avery added **morosely**, "if we don't get going, the end of this lighthouse might be..." She stumbled to find the words.

"A shore thing," finished Evan.

"You mean a sure thing," Ella corrected.

"No," said Evan seriously. "I mean a 'shore enough' disaster." He pulled the crumpled clue list from his pocket once again. "Lady in blue," he said, "check!"

22

THE LEAMINGTON LIGHT

The next morning, the kids got lucky. Mimi was glued to her writing desk overlooking the sea, and John showed up to fetch them in his Jeep.

"Get in!" he said urgently.

The kids scampered into the car, now (for some reason) dusty and muddy, with sand caked in the tire treads.

"You know about the bomb threat," John began. "Well, it's about the old lighthouse, not the one at Harbour Town!"

"We know," said Avery.

John turned around, and the Jeep skidded onto the shoulder of the road. "You know? How do you know?"

"Kids can do research, too, John," Ella said. "Well, Avery did, and we know. We just don't know what to do about it."

"And time is TICKING," Evan added.

"We know, Evan. Quit saying that!" the girls shouted.

John turned back to the road and drove faster than he probably should have around turns through a pine forest. "Evan's right," he said. "There was another clue—I mean note."

"We got one too!" cried the kids, pushing the note up to the front seat over John's shoulder.

"I can't read and drive," he grumbled.

Ella grabbed the piece of paper and read the note aloud:

"YOU KIDS AND YOUR REPORTER FRIEND AND YOUR GRANDMA BETTER STAY OUT OF MY BUSINESS, IF YOU KNOW WHAT'S GOOD FOR YOU!"

John gasped. "How do they know about me? And your grandmother? It doesn't make any sense."

The kids were quiet. Finally Avery said softly, "Maybe it isn't supposed to make sense?"

"You mean like a red herring?" asked Ella, familiar with this kind of trick in one of Mimi's mystery books, where fingers get pointed toward a certain person or thing—just to distract everyone.

"We don't have to eat one, do we?" Evan asked.

"It's not a fish," Avery explained. "It's a literary device."

"A huh-what?" Evan asked. "Is it digital?"

The girls giggled.

"No," said Avery. "It means these clues may not have been to help us solve the mystery, but to keep us as far away from the mystery as possible."

"Well, that's a dirty trick!" complained Evan. "Why would someone do that?"

"To keep us away!" Ella said. "So they can do bad stuff while we are looking elsewhere."

Evan pondered that a minute. "So you mean we have been running around looking for fake clues, and keeping an eye on the candy cane lighthouse, while the bad guy is up to no good somewhere else?"

Avery laughed. "Evan, you couldn't have said it better. Mimi would be proud of your powers of deduction."

Evan frowned. "She'd be prouder if we saved the lighthouse, I think."

"Where are we going, John?" asked Ella, tired of being slung left and right as he zipped around curves.

"Where do you think?" John said. "To the Leamington Light!"

"There are more lighthouses?" asked Ella, astounded.

"No," said John. "Well, yes, but that's neither here nor there right now."

"If they aren't here or there, where are they?" grumbled Evan.

But before John could answer, he skidded the Jeep to a halt. "Stay here!" he ordered in a hateful voice, which surprised the kids.

The kids froze in their seats and stayed put. John opened the back of the Jeep, grabbed a big, heavy-looking backpack, and stalked off without another word.

As he vanished into the pines, Ella said, "That was weird. What's up with him?"

Avery shrugged. "Maybe he's just scared he won't figure this out and get the newspaper the story they want?"

"Why is he mad at us?" Evan asked, a pout on his lips.

Avery patted her brother's shoulder. "It's OK," she assured him. "He needs our help. He just doesn't want to admit it."

Ella shook her head. "Avery, I really don't think Mom, Dad, or Mimi would approve of us getting more involved in this mystery, do you?"

Avery stared out the car window. Evan continued to pout and look afraid. Ella put on her **stern** teacher face.

Finally, Avery said, "You're right, Ella. I agree completely. But here we are." Avery pointed up at the tall, gangly lighthouse towering overhead. "And I don't see anyone else around to do anything."

"John must be trying to do something," Ella reminded her.

Suddenly, Evan yelped, "He is! He is!" He pointed up into the sky. "He's climbing the lighthouse!"

23

A FULL MOON, A THUNDERSTORM

They stared up at John entering the base of the lighthouse, backpack slung over one shoulder.

"So what do we do now?" asked Ella.

"Just wait, I guess," said Evan, plopping down onto a pile of pine straw.

"Look!" cried Avery. "He left his cell phone. I think we should call Mimi to come pick us up."

"And I'm hungry, anyway," grumbled Evan. "And hot. And tired."

For a long time, the kids sat there, watching and waiting. They figured John would get to the top of the lighthouse and then come right back down. It was a tall lighthouse with a lot of steps, so they knew it might take some time. But when Avery saw the sun sinking down behind the pines, she picked up the phone and made the call. Only nothing happened.

"Uh, oh," she said.

"Uh, oh, what?" Ella asked, not liking the sound in her sister's voice.

Avery shook her head. "No service. We must be in a dead zone."

"Don't say DEAD," warned Evan.

"You'd think this big old metal lighthouse might work as a cell tower," said Ella.

"That's not how it works, Ella," said Avery.

"I know," Ella responded dejectedly. "I was just hoping. Now what?"

Suddenly, they spotted something on the balcony near the top of the lighthouse. "John!" they hollered upward, hands cupped to their mouths. "JOHN!" But he either ignored or could not hear them. The wind had whipped up. So had a batch of dark clouds. It began to sprinkle.

In spite of the darkening sky, a full moon could be seen. As the children watched, they spied John enter the top of the lighthouse.

"That thing is a lightning rod," said Evan. And to emphasize the point, a sudden **RUMBLE** of thunder rolled through the night air.

"We'd better get in the Jeep!" urged Avery.

Inside the Jeep, rain spattered the windows so that they could not see the lighthouse well at all, just tall pines waving back and forth in the wind.

"Maybe John's in trouble?" guessed Evan. "Maybe we should go and help him?"

"We don't even have raincoats or umbrellas," Ella fussed.

"And we don't drive either," said Evan. "I certainly don't want to spend the night out here, do you?"

His sisters agreed with him. They found some black plastic garbage bags in the back seat pockets and a pair of scissors in the glove compartment. They hurriedly cut head and arm holes in the bags to make rain gear.

"We look stupid," groused Ella.

"But we'll stay dry," said Avery.

When Evan complained his raincoat was too long, Avery took the scissors and cut the bottom shorter.

"Look!" cried Ella. "John is waving to us!"

Avery peered up through the raindrops. "But is that a 'go away wave' or a 'come help me wave'?" When John vanished back inside the lighthouse, the kids decided they'd better go and help. Maybe they could get cell phone service if they got up higher. Avery stuffed the phone in her pocket.

When the rain ebbed a bit, the kids hopped out of the Jeep and headed toward the lighthouse. Soon, they were wet anyway, and scared...very scared.

24

THE LADY IN BLUE

As quickly as they could, the kids moved forward over slick hills of wet pine straw and through puddles of mud.

"I don't feel good about this," said Avery, when they reached the lighthouse and she opened the door.

"At least it's dry in there," said Ella. She jumped inside.

"And dark," said Evan. "Very dark."

"Our eyes should adjust in a minute," Avery promised as they huddled together. Up high they could hear some metallic noises and a MOAN.

"Maybe John's hurt?" Ella worried.

"Call 911!"

Avery pulled the phone from her pocket and pushed what she thought was 911. In her wet palm, the phone slid away and clanked along the dark floor.

"Come on!" shouted Ella. The kids started up the tall spiral staircase, one careful step at a time.

"GO AWAY!" John suddenly called down to them. "GO AWAY!"

The tone of his voice scared them.

"Maybe there's something dangerous up there?" said Ella.

"Other than lightning?" Evan said, just as a bolt zigzagged overhead.

"The only smart thing to do is to get out of here and back in the car," said Avery. "I'm the oldest and I have to make the decision. It's safety first!"

The others did not argue. They quickly clomped back down the steps and out the door into the rain. As they ran to the car, Evan turned around. "Look! LOOK!"

The girls turned and looked upward. John was outside the lighthouse, clinging to one of the metal legs.

"Why would he do that?" squealed Ella. "Why not come back down the staircase? Is he crazy? And who is THAT?"

Again, the children stared up through the storm to the top of the lighthouse. There on the balcony stood The Lady in Blue, the lighthouse ghost! They screamed and ran for the Jeep!

Before they could reach the car, bright white lights flashed through the trees, poking holes in the darkness. In a moment, a bunch of police cars roared into the clearing. Ignoring the kids, the officers dashed toward the lighthouse. Two more headlights appeared. The car skidded to a halt. A figure hurriedly scrambled out. It was Mimi!

25

USE YOUR HILTON HEAD

"What is going on?!" Mimi cried. She gathered the three wet black bags to her. "I have been so worried!"

"You got our call?" asked Avery. "There was no service."

"Well, there was enough to get through to me and the police, and I tried to call you back, but you didn't answer!" Mimi said, clutching them tightly.

"We were trying to solve the mystery and help John," Evan explained, trying not to cry. "But it's scary in there and we saw..."

"Saw what?" asked Mimi. A look of fear crossed her face.

Ella screamed. "John is hanging off the lighthouse with one hand!"

Everyone looked up, and in the flashes of lightning, they could see that it was true. They also spotted the foxfire-like lights of the police rising up the tower as they climbed the steps to the top of the lighthouse.

Mimi shook her grandchildren. "You don't understand! John is trying to escape!"

"Escape from what?" asked Evan. "Her?"

"Her who?" asked Mimi. "He's trying to escape from the police. John is the bomber—he's the one who made the threat!"

Avery, Ella, and Evan stared at their grandmother, their eyes wide and their mouths open. "WHAT???!!!"

Without another word, Mimi hustled the kids into her car. They climbed in and stared at each other, up at the police rescuing John, and at something blue fluttering down from the top of the lighthouse.

"What's going on?" whispered Evan.

"I don't understand!" said Ella.

But Avery had a determined look on her face. "Think about it," she said. "Use your head. We've been duped, double-crossed, and (she looked like she might cry) we FAILED to solve this mystery!"

26

RESOLUTION

Back at the police station, a wet Mimi, kids, police, and one red-faced reporter stood dripping in the main room.

"You are under arrest for threats against property and persons," the police chief said angrily. He slapped handcuffs on John's wrists and pulled him away to be photographed, fingerprinted, and put into a cell.

The kids were stunned. "We don't understand," said Ella. "What is going on? John is our friend."

A policewoman led them to a table where they all sat down. She brought some dry towels for everyone and a cup of hot coffee for Mimi.

"We only just figured it out ourselves," Officer Adair admitted. "We all know John. He's been a reporter here for years. But then we found out that the article he wrote with the big headline was BEFORE there was any threat!"

"How can that...OH, I get it!" said Evan.

The girls looked at their brother. "You do?" said Avery. "Then please explain it to us!"

They all stared at Evan—even Mimi.

"It was a red ferret," Evan said. "He tricked everyone by making up the whole thing, so no one would think it was him. We were all fooled."

Mimi looked sad. "I've know John so long. He was a character in one of my books. What happened to him? And to think I let him take you around the island. Oh, dear!"

Avery hugged her grandmother. "It's OK, Mimi. We all were tricked. I just don't understand why he bothered to take us around to look up all those clues!"

"OHHHHHH!" cried Mimi. "THE CLUES!"

The kids stared at their grandmother. She didn't seem to know whether to laugh or cry.

"I made up those clues," she admitted.

"YOU DID?" the kids said in shock. "But why?"

Mimi sighed. "I wanted to write a mystery without your help for a change," she admitted. "I thought if I gave you some fake clues, it would keep you occupied. And John volunteered to be part of my little ruse. I'm so sorry!"

"So you red ferreted us, too?" asked Evan. "Shame on you, Mimi." He looked hurt.

All of a sudden, Avery broke out with a big belly laugh.

"What in the world is so funny?" Mimi asked, looking like her feelings were hurt.

"It backfired, Mimi!" she said, giving her grandmother a big hug. "All you did with those clues was lead us into two mysteries—the 'fake clues' one...and the real 'gonna-bomb-the-lighthouse' one."

Mimi looked confused. "So why does that make you laugh?"

"Because," said Avery, "we didn't FAIL on either count. John really did take us around, and we learned a lot about Hilton Head Island and its history. And, if we had not been with him tonight and called you, no one would have known that the lighthouse in question was the REAL Hilton Head Light."

Now Officer Adair laughed. "Have you kids ever thought about being real detectives?" she asked.

Evan tugged off his black bag raincoat and struck a pose. "We ARE real detectives!" he told her.

"Then, Evan," Ella said, "if YOU are a real detective, then you need to learn the difference between a red HERRING and a red FERRET!"

This made everyone laugh, except Evan. His face just got red. But all he really wanted was the last laugh. He went over and whispered in Mimi's ear.

"I don't see why not," she said and gave him a hug. "Seems like a great idea to me!"

"What?" asked Ella, jealous.

"Yeah, what?" repeated Avery, curious.

Even Officer Adair clearly wanted to know what was up. She raised her eyebrows at Mimi, who nodded at Evan.

"See," said Evan, "we have this tradition that we celebrate solving a mystery by going out to eat. So I asked Mimi if we could go to the Hilton Head Diner since it stays open all night!"

"And it has great hamburgers and fries!" added Ella. "Good job, Evan!"

"And delicious chocolate milkshakes!" Avery chimed in. "But do you think we should let Mimi go with us?"

The three kids stared at their grandmother the way she stared at them when they were in trouble.

Finally Evan said, "Well, she can go, but she has to eat red HERRING!"

Mimi laughed and jumped up. "Oh, dear! I was in such a hurry, I think I left the car lights on. I hope the battery isn't dead!"

The kids hurried after their grandmother as she made a dash for the car. On the way, they screamed together, "Mimi, don't use the DEAD WORD!"

27

MYSTERY SOLVED

What happened next?

They all ate a lot at the diner.

John explained that he never planned to really bomb anything. He just wanted a good story so he could get a raise and a promotion. He ended up on probation after the backpack proved to just be filled with blue cloth.

The kids saved what they'd learned from the clues and wrote papers on Hilton Head Island history for school. They all got As.

Mimi decided to retire from doing mysteries (but later changed her mind!).

And the kids were never really sure what they had seen on the top of the lighthouse. Maybe that was a mystery for another day...

The End

Join the Fan Club at
CaroleMarshMysteryClub.com and...

Enter to win
our monthly prize giveaways

1

2
Get status updates
from Mimi and the characters

View the library
of Carole Marsh Mystery titles

3

4
Read
the first 3 chapters of any mystery book for FREE

Download
free activities to go along with your reading adventures!

5

GLOSSARY

bow: (rhymes with wow) the front end of a boat

cleats: metal hooks on a dock that you tie a boat's lines to

harbor: a body of water that offers shelter from rough water for boats, usually in a marina

lines: the nautical term for ropes

marina: docks where boats can tie-up and also get services such as electricity or water

MOB: Man Overboard; if you fall off a boat (or you see someone who does), you should stop the boat and toss them a life ring

PFD: personal flotation device, better known as a life jacket

stern: (noun) the back end of a boat

wake: a stream of white water behind a boat; in a "no wake" zone you are supposed to slow down so a boat's wake cannot cause damage

SAT GLOSSARY

cordon: to block off an area, usually with ropes or tape

morose: sad, dejected, forlorn, down-and-out

parentheses: grammatical marks shaped like this: ( )

ruckus: a racket, disturbance, commotion

stern: (adjective) strict, serious, unsmiling

stoic: to show no emotion